D1634795

Whale tells a tale

Russell Punter

Illustrated by David Semple

Whale is swimming in the sea.

She stops to take a nap.

A gang of sneaky
sharks appears.

They catch
her in a trap.

"You'll be a tasty treat," they cry.
"Don't eat me up!" pleads Whale.

"Please free me and I'll make you rich.
Just listen to my tale..."

While I was floating off the coast,
the breeze became a gale.

*Freezing rain came pounding down
and struck my tail with hail.*

Thunder crashed!
Forked lightning flashed.

I felt the storm winds blow.

Mighty rocks lay dead ahead.
I dived down, far below.

There, beneath a coral reef,
a shipwreck came
in sight.

Upon the deck – a treasure chest,
piled high with something bright.

The chest was full of golden coins
from all around the world.

Out shot a spotted octopus.

This chest belongs to me!

He clung so tight, with all his might,
I couldn't pull it free.

The sharks all grin. "Why, thank you, Whale. We're sure we'd get a hold."

The sharks soon start a fight.

They lift the lid.

Oh no!

No gold!

"Well, what a trick!" they wail.

About phonics

Phonics is a method of teaching reading which is used extensively in today's schools. At its heart is an emphasis on identifying the *sounds* of letters, or combinations of letters, that are then put together to make words. These sounds are known as phonemes.

Starting to read

Learning to read is an important milestone for any child. The process can begin well before children start to learn letters and put them together to read words. The sooner children can discover books and enjoy stories and language, the better they will be prepared for reading themselves, first with the help of an adult and then independently.

You can find out more about phonics on the Usborne website at **usborne.com/Phonics**

Phonemic awareness

An important early stage in pre-reading and early reading is developing phonemic awareness: that is, listening out for the sounds within words. Rhymes, rhyming stories and alliteration are excellent ways of encouraging phonemic awareness.

In this story, your child will soon identify the *a* sound, as in **whale** and **tale.** Look out, too, for rhymes such as **nap – trap** and **hold – gold**.

Hearing your child read

If your child is reading a story to you, don't rush to correct mistakes, but be ready to prompt or guide if he or she is struggling. Above all, do give plenty of praise and encouragement.

Edited by Jenny Tyler and Lesley Sims
Designed by Sam Whibley

Reading consultants: Alison Kelly and Anne Washtell

First published in 2022 by Usborne Publishing Ltd., Usborne House, 83-85 Saffron Hill,
London EC1N 8RT, England. usborne.com Copyright © 2022 Usborne Publishing Ltd. The name
Usborne and the Balloon logo are Trade Marks of Usborne Publishing Ltd. All rights reserved.
No part of this publication may be reproduced, stored in a retrieval system or transmitted
in any form or by any means without the prior permission of the publisher. UE.